THE
KITESURFING KID

THE KITESURFING KID GOES TO NEW ZEALAND

ADRIAN STRAIGHT

ILLUSTRATED BY : NATALIE SCHUTT

AuthorHouse™
1663 Liberty Drive
Bloomington, IN 47403
www.authorhouse.com
Phone: 1 (800) 839-8640

Published by AuthorHouse 04/29/2016

ISBN: 978-1-5246-0463-9 (sc)
ISBN: 978-1-5246-0464-6 (e)

Library of Congress Control Number: 2016906716

Print information available on the last page.

Any people depicted in stock imagery provided by Thinkstock are models,
and such images are being used for illustrative purposes only.
Certain stock imagery © Thinkstock.

This book is printed on acid-free paper.

Because of the dynamic nature of the Internet, any web addresses or links contained in this book may have changed
since publication and may no longer be valid. The views expressed in this work are solely those of the author and do not
necessarily reflect the views of the publisher, and the publisher hereby disclaims any responsibility for them.

authorHOUSE°

This is a tale about journey and adventure,

so listen closely, and we will go venture.

There once was a boy who flew a big kite.

He would ride on a board all day and all night.

He wandered and flew wherever the wind blew,

sailing across the ocean blue.

When he was a baby, he'd discovered the wind,

as he tried to walk with a big grin.

He would fall and laugh with each big puff,

never seeming to get enough.

Before he could run, a kite was in hand,

sailing his flag all over the sand.

As hyper as a bee and turning three,

he hopped on a board and started bending his knees.

Making monumental decisions at the age of five,

he said, "I need to see the world to feel alive."

The time of year was good but not quite perfect,

so he waited for the weather and prepared to take flight.

He sailed to the west and started his journey

through the waves and the wind forever yearning.

After days of kiting, he finally found land,

gliding in from the northeast, right up to the sand.

There were volcanic rocks jutting out from the deep,

with all sorts of birds perched high on their peak.

Snow-capped mountains lined the east,

with peaks ever so steep.

All sorts of birds were ready to swoop;

the falcons above drew a big loop.

Falling and diving as fast as it could,

it goes for a *Kawekaweau** that hid under some wood

with great-big claws and a powerful beak;

the Kawekaweau scrambled for a small creek.

It dove into a burrow buried under some grass,

just as the falcon was making a pass.

The falcon knew he was not coming out,

so he went on looking and flying about.

* Kawekaweau: Maori term for a giant forest gecko

The sun fell fast as the moon rose,

and this was when our hero struck a pose.

He looked to the mountains and back to the sea,

wondering where he should sleep—maybe under a tree.

Using his kite and whatever he could find,

he started building a shelter that was one of a kind.

He then built a fire that rose to the sky,

when suddenly a shooting star went flying by!

As he looked into the night sky above,

the universe opened up and showed him some love.

With a twinkle of brightness ever so bright,

three stars up above gave him a great sight.

There were snow-capped mountains and rivers running deep.

The land and sea were silent with all the animals going to sleep.

The waves crashed loudly, and the sea was alive;

as the waves subsided, he noticed a beehive.

They seemed to be drowsy because of the campfire,

so the boy lay down as he began to retire.

Before long, the fire soothed him to sleep;

not until the morning did he make even a peep.

Before the sun was in the sky,

he was in the water, watching the fish swim by.

He dove to some depths and pried off a rock

a shellfish named *paua*,* which he put in his sock.

After picking a few, he'd had enough;

he'd better swim in before the seas become rough.

* Paua: Maori term for abalone

After cutting and cleaning his paua catch,

he dug into the roots of a pretty white flower patch.

With his nose smelling something sweet,

he just knew that he was in for a delicious treat.

The roots of the flower presented their beauty,

with bunches of little white *riki** showing their true duty.

* Riki: Maori term for onion

After cooking up and eating a feast,

he then gazed out, looking to the east.

As the sun began to show itself to the dark and cold night,

the boy got up and started to take flight.

He broke down his camp and cleaned up his gear,

so that only footprints and paua shells were left to appear.

Giving his kite some fresh air while feeling the breeze,

he was hoping the weather was not being a tease.

Sometimes the wind is fickle and will stop blowing,

at which point your body does all the towing.

Swimming and sailing with the kite in the water,

he patiently waited for the wind to blow harder.

He went to the east and followed the wind,

for his journey around the world was about to begin.

The wind began to howl as frothy peaks formed,

almost as if there was a brewing storm.

He rode a bit longer before seeing some land;

he was so far away, he could barely see the island sand.

As the rain began to fall, the winds started to turn,

and the boy saw a small cove sheltered by a big berm.

He barely made it to shore

as the rain began to pour.

Lightning struck a palm close by,

giving the coconuts a bit of a fry.

Under some trees with his kite propped fast,

he waited for the storm to finally pass.

When the storm finally passed, guess what remained?

A giant rainbow appeared because it had rained.

It was not until dawn when the rain stopped falling,

as the sun rose up and the birds started calling.

The storm brought the rain, which made the rivers grow.

As the water started to ebb, the banks were aglow.

There were many *Kutai** and *Tio** exposed by the flow,

because the banks got washed out, and now the mollusks*

started to show.

* Kutai: Maori term for mussels

* Tio: Maori term for oysters

* Mollusks: a large group of animals that have soft bodies,

lack a backbone, and usually live in a shell

After building a fire from debris and flint rocks,

he scrambled across the bank to join the flocks.

The kitesurfing kid grabbed as many as he could carry

and walked them back to his camp, where his fire was as red

as a cherry.

The fire was lined with flat rocks around,

to keep the delicious food high off of the ground.

After sizzling and bubbling, the Kutai started to move,

opening up their shells as the boy started to groove.

The Tio as well cooked open their shells,

as the camp filled with delicious smells.

The boy dug in and started to eat;

he ate every bite, enjoying his treat.

He looked to the sky and smelled the air around.

The air was so fresh, and the leaves were aground.

The storm had blown past, and you know what that means:

the wind will come fast and blow through the trees.

It was time to set up and get ready to fly.

It has come to that time where he had to say good-bye.

Cleaning up his camp and leaving nothing but footprints on the land,

he gave his chest a bump and said *whakawhetai koe** and stretched out his hand.

He then felt a gust and looked to the sea.

There were whitecaps and waves as far as he could see.

* Whakawhetai Koe: Maori term for thank you

Walking out to the water with his kite in his hand,

he wondered if he could make it over to Thailand.

With a grin on his face and wind at his back,

our kitesurfing kid began his first tack.

About the Author

Adrian Straight was born and raised in California and has been kitesurfing most of his life. He traveled to New Zealand after graduating from University of California, Santa Barbara, with a degree in hydrology. It was such a magical place that our author was inspired to write an educational children's book based on his travels and the local culture of New Zealand. He now resides in Southern California, where he is a substitute teacher, swim coach, and entrepreneurial landscaper during the calm days and a kitesurfer on any windy days.

About the Illustrator

Natalie Schutt is a SoCal-grown, ocean-loving, fine art wedding photographer and artist. Her passion for painting and photography began at a young age, and really flourished after she graduated from the California Polytechnic State University of San Luis Obispo, where she sought after her dream of doing something creative every day. She was also introduced to swimming and surfing growing up, living right along the coast of California. The ocean is seriously a magical place: a place where inner growth is amplified. She feels truly blessed to continually be shaped by the ocean and its wonders, and to be able to pursue an artistic passion for a living.